The Cats of Ulthar

Lovecraft, Howard Phillips

Published: 1920

About Lovecraft:

Howard Phillips Lovecraft was an American author of fantasy, horror and science fiction. He is notable for blending elements of science fiction and horror; and for popularizing "cosmic horror": the notion that some concepts, entities or experiences are barely comprehensible to human minds, and those who delve into such risk their sanity. Lovecraft has become a cult figure in the horror genre and is noted as creator of the "Cthulhu Mythos," a series of loosely interconnected fictions featuring a "pantheon" of nonhuman creatures, as well as the famed Necronomicon, a grimoire of magical rites and forbidden lore. His works typically had a tone of "cosmic pessimism," regarding mankind as insignificant and powerless in the universe. Lovecraft's readership was limited during his life, and his works, particularly early in his career, have been criticized as occasionally ponderous, and for their uneven quality. Nevertheless, Lovecraft's reputation has grown tremendously over the decades, and he is now commonly regarded as one of the most important horror writers of the 20th Century, exerting an influence that is widespread, though often indirect.

It is said that in Ulthar, which lies beyond the river Skai, no man may kill a cat; and this I can verily believe as I gaze upon him who sitteth purring before the fire. For the cat is cryptic, and close to strange things which men cannot see. He is the soul of antique Aegyptus, and bearer of tales from forgotten cities in Meroe and Ophir. He is the kin of the jungle's lords, and heir to the secrets of hoary and sinister Africa. The Sphinx is his cousin, and he speaks her language; but he is more ancient than the Sphinx, and remembers that which she hath forgotten.

In Ulthar, before ever the burgesses forbade the killing of cats, there dwelt an old cotter and his wife who delighted to trap and slay the cats of their neighbors. Why they did this I know not; save that many hate the voice of the cat in the night, and take it ill that cats should run stealthily about yards and gardens at twilight. But whatever the reason, this old man and woman took pleasure in trapping and slaying every cat which came near to their hovel; and from some of the sounds heard after dark, many villagers fancied that the manner of slaying was exceedingly peculiar. But the villagers did not discuss such things with the old man and his wife; because of the habitual expression on the withered faces of the two, and because their cottage was so small and so darkly hidden under spreading oaks at the back of a neglected yard. In truth, much as the owners of cats hated these odd folk, they feared them more; and instead of berating them as brutal assassins, merely took care that no cherished pet or mouser should stray toward the remote hovel under the dark trees. When through some unavoidable oversight a cat was missed, and sounds heard after dark, the loser would lament impotently; or console himself by thanking Fate that it was not one of his children who had thus vanished. For the people of Ulthar were simple, and knew not whence it is all cats first came.

One day a caravan of strange wanderers from the South entered the narrow cobbled streets of Ulthar. Dark wanderers they were, and unlike the other roving folk who passed through the village twice every year. In the market-place they told fortunes for silver, and bought gay beads from the merchants. What was the land of these wanderers none could tell; but it was seen that they were given to strange prayers, and that they had painted on the sides of their wagons strange figures with human bodies and the heads of cats, hawks, rams and lions. And the leader of the caravan wore a headdress with two horns and a curious disk betwixt the horns.

There was in this singular caravan a little boy with no father or mother, but only a tiny black kitten to cherish. The plague had not been kind to him, yet had left him this small furry thing to mitigate his sorrow; and when one is very young, one can find great relief in the lively antics of a black kitten. So the boy whom the dark people called Menes smiled more often than he wept as he sat playing with his graceful kitten on the steps of an oddly painted wagon.

On the third morning of the wanderers' stay in Ulthar, Menes could not find his kitten; and as he sobbed aloud in the market-place certain villagers told him of the old man and his wife, and of sounds heard in the night. And when he heard these things his sobbing gave place to meditation, and finally to prayer. He stretched out his arms toward the sun and prayed in a tongue no villager could understand; though indeed the villagers did not try very hard to understand, since their attention was mostly taken up by the sky and the odd shapes the clouds were assuming. It was very peculiar, but as the little boy uttered his petition there seemed to form overhead the shadowy, nebulous figures of exotic things; of hybrid creatures crowned with horn-flanked disks. Nature is full of such illusions to impress the imaginative.

That night the wanderers left Ulthar, and were never seen again. And the householders were troubled when they noticed that in all the village there was not a cat to be found. From each hearth the familiar cat had vanished; cats large and small, black, grey, striped, yellow and white. Old Kranon, the burgo-master, swore that the dark folk had taken the cats away in revenge for the killing of Menes' kitten; and cursed the caravan and the little boy. But Nith, the lean notary, declared that the old cotter and his wife were more likely persons to suspect; for their hatred of cats was notorious and increasingly bold. Still, no one durst complain to the sinister couple; even when little Atal, the innkeeper's son, vowed that he had at twilight seen all the cats of Ulthar in that accursed yard under the trees, pacing very slowly and solemnly in a circle around the cottage, two abreast, as if in performance of some unheard-of rite of beasts. The villagers did not know how much to believe from so small a boy; and though they feared that the evil pair had charmed the cats to their death, they preferred not to chide the old cotter till they met him outside his dark and repellent yard.

So Ulthar went to sleep in vain anger; and when the people awakened at dawn - behold! every cat was back at his accustomed hearth! Large and small, black, grey, striped, yellow and white, none was missing. Very sleek and fat did the cats appear, and sonorous with purring content. The citizens talked with one another of the affair, and marveled not a little. Old Kranon again insisted that it was the dark folk who had taken them, since cats did not return alive from the cottage of the ancient man and his wife. But all agreed on one thing: that the refusal of all the cats to eat their portions of meat or drink their saucers of milk was exceedingly curious. And for two whole days the sleek, lazy cats of Ulthar would touch no food, but only doze by the fire or in the sun.

It was fully a week before the villagers noticed that no lights were appearing at dusk in the windows of the cottage under the trees. Then the lean Nith remarked that no one had seen the old man or his wife since the night the cats were away. In another week the burgomaster decided to overcome his fears and call at the strangely silent dwelling as a matter of duty, though in so doing he was careful to take with him Shang the blacksmith and Thul the cutter of stone as witnesses. And when they had broken down the frail door they found only this: two cleanly picked human skeletons on the earthen floor, and a number of singular beetles crawling in the shadowy corners.

There was subsequently much talk among the burgesses of Ulthar. Zath, the coroner, disputed at length with Nith, the lean notary; and Kranon and Shang and Thul were overwhelmed with questions. Even little Atal, the innkeeper's son, was closely questioned and given a sweetmeat as reward. They talked of the old cotter and his wife, of the caravan of dark wanderers, of small Menes and his black kitten, of the prayer of Menes and of the sky during that prayer, of the doings of the cats on the night the caravan left, and of what was later found in the cottage under the dark trees in the repellent yard.

And in the end the burgesses passed that remarkable law which is told of by traders in Hatheg and discussed by travelers in Nir; namely, that in Ulthar no man may kill a cat.

Biography & Bibliography

Howard Phillips Lovecraft (August 20, 1890 – March 15, 1937) was an American writer who achieved posthumous fame through his influential works of horror fiction. He was virtually unknown and published only in pulp magazines before he died in poverty, but he is now regarded as one of the most significant 20th-century authors in his genre.

Lovecraft was born in Providence, Rhode Island, where he spent most of his life. Among his most celebrated tales are "The Rats in the Walls", "The Call of Cthulhu", At the Mountains of Madness and The Shadow Out of Time, all canonical to the Cthulhu Mythos. Lovecraft was never able to support himself from earnings as an author and editor. He saw commercial success increasingly elude him in this latter period, partly because he lacked the confidence and drive to promote himself. He subsisted in progressively strained circumstances in his last years; an inheritance was completely spent by the time he died, at age 46.

Biography

Early life (1890-1908)

Lovecraft was born in his family home on August 20, 1890, in Providence, Rhode Island. He was the only child of Winfield Scott Lovecraft (1853–1898) and Sarah Susan (Susie) Phillips Lovecraft (1857–1921). Though his employment is hard to discern, Lovecraft's future wife, Sonia Greene, stated that Winfield was employed by Gorham Manufacturing Company as a traveling salesman. Susie's family was of substantial means at the time of their marriage; her father, Whipple Van Buren Phillips, being involved in many significant business ventures. In April 1893, after a psychotic episode in a Chicago hotel, Winfield was committed to Butler Hospital in Providence. Though it is not clear who reported Winfield's prior behavior to Butler, medical records indicate that he had been "doing and saying strange things at times" for a year before his commitment. Winfield spent five years in Butler before dying in 1898. His death certificate listed the cause of death as general paresis, a term synonymous with late-stage syphilis. Susie never exhibited symptoms of the disease, leading to questions regarding the intimacy of their relationship. In 1969 Sonia Greene ventured that Susie was a "touch-me-not" wife and that Winfield, being a traveling salesmen, "took his sexual pleasures wherever he could find them". How Greene came to this opinion is unknown, as she never met Lovecraft's parents, though Lovecraft himself termed his mother a "touch-me-not" in a 1937 letter noting that, after his early childhood, she avoided all physical contact with him. This is contrary to Susie's treatment of a young Lovecraft soon after his father's breakdown. According to the accounts of family friends Susie doted over the young Lovecraft to a fault, pampering him and never letting him out of her sight. Throughout his life Lovecraft maintained that his father fell into a paralytic state, due to insomnia and being overworked, and remained that way until his death. It is unknown if Lovecraft was simply kept ignorant of his father's illness or if his later remarks were intentionally misleading.

After his father's hospitalization, Lovecraft resided in the family home with his mother, his maternal aunts Lillian and Annie, and his maternal grandparents Whipple and Robie. Lovecraft later recollected that after his father's illness his mother was "permanently stricken with grief." Whipple became a father figure to Lovecraft in this time, Lovecraft noting that his grandfather became the "centre of my entire universe." Whipple, who traveled often on business, maintained correspondence with the young Lovecraft by letter who, by the age of three, was already proficient at reading and writing. When home Whipple would share weird tales of his own invention and show Lovecraft objects of art he had acquired in his European travels. Lovecraft also credits Whipple with being instrumental in overcoming his fear of the dark when Whipple forced Lovecraft, at five years old, to walk through several darkened rooms in the family home. It was in this period that Lovecraft was introduced to some of his earliest literary influences such as The Rime of the Ancient Mariner illustrated by Doré, One Thousand and One Nights, a gift from his mother, Thomas Bulfinch's Age of Fable and Ovid's Metamorphoses.

While there is no indication that Lovecraft was particularly close to his grandmother Robie, her death in 1896 had a profound effect. By his own account, it sent his family into "a gloom from which it never fully recovered." His mother and aunts' wearing of black mourning dresses "terrified" him, and it is at this time that Lovecraft, approximately five and half years old, started having nightmares that would inform his later writing. Specifically, he began to have recurring nightmares of beings he termed "night-gaunts"; their appearance he credited to the influence of Doré's illustrations, which would "whirl me through space at a sickening rate of speed, the while fretting & impelling me with their detestable tridents." Thirty years later night gaunts would appear in Lovecraft's writing.

Lovecraft's earliest known literary works began at age seven with poems restyling the Odyssey and other mythological stories. Lovecraft has said that as a child he was enamored with the Roman pantheon of gods, accepting them as genuine expressions of divinity and foregoing his Christian upbringing. He recalls, at five years old, being told Santa Claus didn't exist and retorting by asking why "God is not equally a myth?" At the age of eight he took a keen interest in the sciences, particularly astronomy and chemistry. He also examined the anatomy books available to him in the family library, learning the specifics of human reproduction that had yet to be explained to him, and found that it "virtually killed my interest in the subject." In 1902, according to Lovecraft's own correspondence, astronomy became a guiding influence on his world view. He began producing the periodical Rhode Island Journal of Astronomy, of which 69 issues survive, using the hectograph printing method. Lovecraft went in and out of elementary school repeatedly, oftentimes with home tutors making up for those lost school years, missing time due to health concerns that are not entirely clear. The written recollections of his peers described him as both withdrawn yet openly welcoming to anyone who shared his current fascination with astronomy, inviting anyone to look through the telescope he prized.

By 1900 Whipple's various business concerns were suffering a downturn and slowly reducing his family's wealth. He was forced to let the family's hired servants go, leaving Lovecraft, Whipple and Susie, being the only unmarried sister, alone in the family home. In the spring of 1904 Whipple's largest business venture suffered a catastrophic failure. Within months he died due to a stroke at age 70. After Whipple's death Susie was unable to support the upkeep of the expansive family home on what remained of the Phillips' estate. Later that year she was forced to move herself and her son to a small duplex. Lovecraft has called this time one of the darkest of his life, remarking in a 1934 letter that he saw no point in living anymore. In fall of the same year he started high school. Much like his earlier school years, Lovecraft was at times removed from school for long periods for what he termed "near breakdowns". He did say, though, that while having some conflicts with teachers, he enjoyed high school, becoming close with a small circle of friends. Aside from a pause in 1904 he also resumed publishing the Rhode Island Journal of Astronomy as well as starting the Scientific Gazette, which dealt mostly with chemistry. It was also during this period that Lovecraft produced the first of the types of fiction he would later be known for, namely "The Beast in the Cave" and "The Alchemist".

It was in 1908, prior to his high school graduation, when Lovecraft suffered another health crisis of some sort, though this instance was seemingly more severe than any prior. The exact circumstances and causes remain unknown. The only direct records are Lovecraft's own later correspondence wherein he described it variously as a "nervous collapse" and "a sort of breakdown", in one letter blaming it on the stress of high school despite his enjoying it. In another letter concerning the events of 1908 he notes, "I was and am prey to intense headaches, insomnia, and general nervous weakness which prevents my continuous application to anything." Though Lovecraft maintained that he was to attend Brown University after high school, he never graduated and never attended school again. Whether Lovecraft suffered from a physical ailment, a mental one, or some combination thereof has never been determined. An account from a high school classmate described Lovecraft as exhibiting "terrible tics" and that at times "he'd be sitting in his seat and he'd suddenly up and jump." Harry Brobst, who recorded the account and had a Ph.D. in psychology, claimed that chorea minor was the most likely cause of Lovecraft's childhood symptoms while noting that instances of chorea minor after adolescence are very rare. Lovecraft himself acknowledged in letters that he suffered from bouts of chorea as a child. Brobst further ventured that Lovecraft's 1908 breakdown was attributed to a "hysteroid seizure", a term that today usually denotes atypical depression. In another letter concerning the events of 1908, Lovecraft stated that he "could hardly bear to see or speak to anyone, & liked to shut out the world by pulling down dark shades & using artificial light."

Earliest recognition (1908-1914)

Not much of Lovecraft and Susie's activities from late 1908 to 1913 are recorded. Lovecraft mentions a steady continuation of their financial decline highlighted by a failed business venture of his uncle that cost Susie a large portion of their dwindling wealth. Accounts differ on how reclusive Susie and Lovecraft were during this time. A friend of Susie, Clara Hess, recalled a visit during which Susie spoke continuously about Lovecraft being "so hideous that he hid from everyone and did not like to walk upon the streets where people could gaze on him." Despite Hess' protest that this wasn't the case, Susie maintained this stance. In the same account though, Hess said she regularly saw Susie out and about riding streetcars.

For his part, Lovecraft said he found his mother to be "a positive marvel of consideration." A next-door neighbor later pointed out that what others in the neighborhood often supposed were loud, nocturnal quarrels between mother and son, she recognized as being recitations of Shakespeare; an activity that seemed to delight mother and son. Susie had an adoration for French literature, having studied French in boarding school. Lovecraft, though he never matched his mother's admiration of French literature, admired her knowledge and devotion to it. Lovecraft recalls Susie also had a passion for painting landscapes of the surrounding countryside, though none of her work survives today. One of Lovecraft's later friends, C. M. Eddy Jr., became aware of Lovecraft due to his wife Muriel, whose mother-in-law attended a women's suffrage meeting where she met Susie.

During this period Lovecraft revived his earlier scientific periodicals. He endeavored to commit himself to the study of organic chemistry, Susie buying the expensive glass chemistry assemblage he wanted. Lovecraft found his studies were hobbled by the mathematics involved, which he found boring and would cause headaches that would incapacitate him for a day. Lovecraft's first poem that wasn't self-published appeared in a local newspaper in 1912. Called "Providence in 2000 A.D.", the poem envisioned a future where proper people of English heritage were displaced by immigrants. Surviving unpublished poems from this period, most notoriously "On the Creation of Niggers", were also emblematic of the xenophobia and racism inherent in much of Lovecraft's later work.

In 1911 Lovecraft's letters to editors began appearing in pulp and weird fiction magazines, most notably Argosy. A 1913 letter critical of Fred Jackson, a prominent writer for Argosy, started Lovecraft down a path that would greatly affect his life. Lovecraft described Jackson's stories as "trivial, effeminate, and, in places, coarse." Continuing, Lovecraft said that Jackson's characters exhibit the "delicate passions and emotions proper to negroes and anthropoid apes." This sparked a nearly year-long feud in the letters section of Argosy between Lovecraft, along with his occasional supporters, and the majority of readers critical of his view of Jackson. Lovecraft's biggest critic was John Russell, who often replied in verse, and to whom Lovecraft felt compelled to reply to because he respected Russell's writing skills. The most immediate effect of the feud was the recognition garnered from Edward F. Daas, then head editor of the United Amateur Press Association. Daas invited Russell and Lovecraft to the organization and both accepted, Lovecraft in April 1914.

Rejuvenation and tragedy (1914-1921)

Lovecraft immersed himself in the world of amateur journalism for most of the following decade. During this period he was an advocate for amateurism versus commercialism. Lovecraft's definition of commercialism, though, was specific to writing for, what he considered, low-brow publications for pay. He contrasted this with his view of "professional publication", which he termed as writing for journals and publishers he considered respectable. He thought of amateur journalism as training and practice for a professional career. Lovecraft was appointed to chairman of the Department of Public Criticism of the UAPA in late 1914. He used this position to advocate for his, what many considered peculiar, insistence on the superiority of English language usage that most writers already considered archaic. Emblematic of the Anglophile opinions he maintained throughout his life, he openly criticized other UAPA contributors for their "Americanisms" and "slang". Often these criticisms were couched in xenophobic and racist arguments bemoaning the "bastardization" of the "national language" by immigrants. In mid-1915 Lovecraft was elected to the position of first vice-president of the UAPA. Two years later he was elected president and appointed other board members that mostly shared his view on the supremacy of classical English over modern American English. Another significant event of this time was the beginning of World War I. Lovecraft published multiple criticisms of the US government's, and the American public's reluctance to join the war to protect England, which he viewed as the America's homeland.

In 1916 Lovecraft published his early short story "The Alchemist" in the main UAPA journal, a departure from his usual verse. Due in no small part to the encouragement of W. Paul Cook, another UAPA member and future life-long friend, Lovecraft began writing and publishing more fiction. Soon to follow were "The Tomb" and "Dagon". "The Tomb", by Lovecraft's own admission, follows closely the style and construction of the writings of one of his largest influences, Edgar Allan Poe. "Dagon" though, is considered Lovecraft's first work that embraced the concepts and themes that his writing would later be known for. In 1918 Lovecraft's term as president of the UAPA elapsed, and he took his former post as chairman of the Department of Public Criticism. In 1919 Lovecraft published another short story, "Beyond the Wall of Sleep".

In 1917 came two first-hand accounts suggesting that, despite his climb in the ranks of the UAPA, Lovecraft still lived a fairly hermetical life. One comes from Cook himself, the other Rheinhart Kleiner, a Brooklyn-based UAPA writer. Both recalled that during their visits Lovecraft's mother regularly checked in on Lovecraft. Kleiner mentioned that "at every hour or so his mother appeared in the doorway with a glass of milk, and Lovecraft forthwith drank it." In the same account Kleiner described Susie as "very cordial and even vivacious." Cook recounts an almost comical delay of his meeting with Lovecraft wherein Susie and Lillian wouldn't let Cook in because Lovecraft had been up all night writing and couldn't be disturbed. Eventually Lovecraft appeared at the door in his "dressing gown and slippers." Lovecraft later attributed his mother and aunt's reticence to allow Cook in being due to his unkempt appearance and their general dislike of Lovecraft's involvement with amateur journalism. Also in 1917, as Lovecraft related to Kleiner, was Lovecraft's aborted attempt to enlist in the army. Though he passed the physical exam, he told Kleiner that his mother "has threatened to go to any lengths, legal or otherwise, if I do not reveal all the ills which unfit me for the army."

In the winter of 1918–1919, Susie, exhibiting symptoms of a "nervous breakdown" of some sort, went to live with her elder sister Lillian. It is unclear what Susie may have been suffering from. Clara Hess, interviewed decades later, recalled instances of Susie describing "weird and fantastic creatures that rushed out from behind buildings and from corners at dark." In the same account Hess describes a time when they crossed paths in downtown Providence and Susie "was excited and

13

apparently did not know where she was." Whatever the causes, in March 1919 they resulted in Susie being committed to Butler Hospital, like her husband before her. Lovecraft's immediate reaction to Susie's commitment was visceral, writing to Kleiner that, "existence seems of little value," and that he wished "it might terminate." Speaking to Susie's doctors, a month after she entered Butler, Lovecraft came to the realization that she was never going to be released.

The nature of Susie's illness is impossible to ascertain. Her medical records were lost in a fire, and the only Lovecraft researcher to have seen them prior was Winfield Townley Scott. His account describes Susie weeping often and speaking regularly about both her family's financial collapse and her son, whom she described as "a poet of the highest order." Her psychiatrist claimed she had Oedipus complex. The psychiatric views of the day, still beholden to archaic Victorian assumptions, make any contemporary diagnosis of Susie questionable. No matter their symptoms or situations, women were predominately diagnosed (as Susie was) with hysteria, a concept that women are inherently mentally frail due to having "thinner blood" as result of menstruation and having a uterus. Lovecraft visited Susie often, walking the large grounds with her, and sent her letters on a regular basis.

Late 1919 saw Lovecraft become more outgoing. After a period of isolation, he began joining friends in trips to writer gatherings, the first being a talk in Boston presented by Lord Dunsany, whom Lovecraft recently discovered and idolized. In early 1920, at an amateur writer convention, he met Frank Belknap Long, who would end up being Lovecraft's most influential and closest confidant for the rest of his life. This period also proved to be the most prolific of Lovecraft's short-story career. The influence of Dunsany is readily apparent in his 1919 output, later be to coined Lovecraft's Dream Cycle, with stories like "The White Ship", "The Doom that Came to Sarnath", and "The Statement of Randolph Carter". In early 1920 followed "Celephais" and "The Cats of Ulthar". It was later in 1920 that Lovecraft began publishing the earliest stories that fit into the Cthulhu Mythos. The Cthulhu Mythos, a term coined by August Derleth, encompasses Lovecraft's stories that share a commonality in fictional locations and Lovecraft's invented pantheon of god-like beings known as The Great Old Ones. The poem "Nyarlathotep" and short story "The Crawling Chaos", in collaboration with Winifred Virginia Jackson, were written in late 1920. Following in early 1921 came "The Nameless City", the first story that falls definitively within the Cthulhu Mythos. In it is found one of Lovecraft's most enduring bits of writing, a couplet recited by his creation Abdul Alhazred, "That is not dead which can eternal lie; And with strange aeons even death may die."

On May 24, 1921, Sarah Susan (Susie) Phillips Lovecraft died in Butler Hospital, due to complications from a gall bladder surgery five days earlier. Lovecraft's initial reaction, expressed in a letter nine days after Susie's death, was that of an "extreme nervous shock" that crippled him physically and emotionally, again remarking that he found no reason he should continue living. Despite Lovecraft's immediate reaction to his mother's death, he continued to attend amateur journalist conventions. It was at one such convention in July that Lovecraft met Sonia Greene.

Marriage and New York

Lovecraft's aunts disapproved of this relationship with Sonia. Lovecraft and Greene married on March 3, 1924, and relocated to her Brooklyn apartment at 793 Flatbush Avenue; she thought he needed to get out of Providence in order to flourish and was willing to support him financially. Greene, who had been married before, later said Lovecraft had performed satisfactorily as a lover, though she had to take the initiative in all aspects of the relationship. She attributed Lovecraft's passive nature to a stultifying upbringing by his mother. Lovecraft's weight increased to 90 kg (200 lb) on his wife's home cooking.

He was enthralled by New York, and, in what was informally dubbed the Kalem Club, he acquired a group of encouraging intellectual and literary friends who urged him to submit stories to Weird Tales; editor Edwin Bairdaccepted many otherworldly 'Dream Cycle' Lovecraft stories for the ailing publication, though they were heavily criticized by a section of the readership. Established informally some years before Lovecraft arrived in New York, the core Kalem Club members were boys' adventure novelist Henry Everett McNeil; the lawyer and anarchist writer James Ferdinand Morton, Jr.; and the poet Reinhardt Kleiner.

On New Year's Day of 1925, Sonia moved to Cleveland for a job opportunity, and Lovecraft left Flatbush for a small first-floor apartment on 169 Clinton Street "at the edge of Red Hook"—a location which came to discomfort him greatly. Later that year the Kalem Club's four regular attendees were joined by Lovecraft along with his protégé Frank Belknap Long, bookseller George Willard Kirk, and Lovecraft's close friend Samuel Loveman. Loveman was Jewish, but was unaware of Lovecraft's nativist attitudes. Conversely, it has been suggested that Lovecraft, who disliked mention of sexual matters, was unaware that Loveman and some of his other friends were homosexual.

Financial difficulties

Not long after the marriage, Greene lost her business and her assets disappeared in a bank failure; she also became ill. Lovecraft made efforts to support his wife through regular jobs, but his lack of previous work experience meant he lacked proven marketable skills. After a few unsuccessful spells as a low-level clerk, his job-seeking became desultory. The publisher of Weird Tales attempted to put the loss-making magazine on a business footing and offered the job of editor to Lovecraft, who declined, citing his reluctance to relocate to Chicago; "think of the tragedy of such a move for an aged antiquarian," the 34-year-old writer declared. Baird was replaced with Farnsworth Wright, whose writing Lovecraft had criticized. Lovecraft's submissions were often rejected by Wright. (This may have been partially due to censorship guidelines imposed in the aftermath of a Weird Tales story that hinted at necrophilia, although after Lovecraft's death Wright accepted many of the stories he had originally rejected.)

Brooklyn

Greene, moving where the work was, relocated to Cincinnati, and then to Cleveland; her employment required constant travel. Added to the daunting reality of failure in a city with a large immigrant population, Lovecraft's single-room apartment at 169 Clinton Street in Brooklyn Heights, not far from the working-class waterfront neighborhood Red Hook, was burgled, leaving him with only the clothes he was wearing. In August 1925 he wrote "The Horror at Red Hook" and "He", in the latter of which the narrator says "My coming to New York had been a mistake; for whereas I had looked for poignant wonder and inspiration ... I had found instead only a sense of horror and oppression which threatened to master, paralyze, and annihilate me". It was at around this time he wrote the outline for "The Call of Cthulhu", with its theme of the insignificance of all humanity. In the bibliographical study H. P. Lovecraft: Against the World, Against Life, Michel Houellebecq suggested that the misfortunes fed Lovecraft's central motivation as a writer, which he said was racial resentment. With a weekly allowance Greene sent, Lovecraft moved to a working-class area of Brooklyn Heights, where he subsisted in a tiny apartment. He had lost 40 pounds (18 kg) of body weight by 1926, when he left for Providence.

Return to Providence

Back in Providence, Lovecraft lived in a "spacious brown Victorian wooden house" at 10 Barnes Street until 1933. The same address is given as the home of Dr. Willett in Lovecraft's The Case of Charles Dexter Ward. The period beginning after his return to Providence—the last decade of his life— was Lovecraft's most prolific; in that time he produced short stories, as well as his longest work of fiction The Case of Charles Dexter Ward and At the Mountains of Madness. He frequently revised work for other authors and did a large amount of ghost-writing, including "The Mound", "Winged Death", and "The Diary of Alonzo Typer". Client Harry Houdini was laudatory, and attempted to help Lovecraft by introducing him to the head of a newspaper syndicate. Plans for a further project were ended by Houdini's death.

Although he was able to combine his distinctive style (allusive and amorphous description by horrified though passive narrators) with the kind of stock content and action that the editor of Weird Tales wanted—Wright paid handsomely to snap up "The Dunwich Horror" which proved very popular with readers—Lovecraft increasingly produced work that brought him no remuneration. Affecting a calm indifference to the reception of his works, Lovecraft was in reality extremely sensitive to criticism and easily precipitated into withdrawal. He was known to give up trying to sell a story after it had been once rejected. Sometimes, as with The Shadow Over Innsmouth (which included a rousing chase that supplied action) he wrote a story that might have been commercially viable, but did not try to sell it. Lovecraft even ignored interested publishers. He failed to reply when one inquired about any novel Lovecraft might have ready: although he had completed such a work, The Case of Charles Dexter Ward, it was never typed up.

A few years after Lovecraft had moved to Providence, he and his wife Sonia Greene, having been living separately for so long, agreed to an amicable divorce. Greene moved to California in 1933 and remarried in 1936, unaware that Lovecraft, despite his assurances to the contrary, had never officially signed the final decree.

Last years

Lovecraft was never able to provide even basic expenses by selling stories and doing paid literary work for others. He lived frugally, subsisting on an inheritance that was nearly depleted by the time he died. He sometimes went without food to be able to pay the cost of mailing letters. Eventually, he was forced to move to meager lodgings with his surviving aunt. He was also deeply affected by the suicide of his correspondent Robert E. Howard. In early 1937, he was diagnosed with cancer of the small intestine and suffered from malnutrition as a result. He lived in constant pain until his death on March 15, 1937 in Providence. In accordance with his lifelong scientific curiosity, he kept a diary of his illness until close to the moment of his death.

Lovecraft was listed along with his parents on the Phillips family monument (41°51′14″N 71°22′52″W). In 1977, fans erected a headstone in Swan Point Cemetery on which they inscribed his name, the dates of his birth and death, and the phrase "I AM PROVIDENCE"—a line from one of his personal letters.

Groups of enthusiasts annually observe the anniversaries of Lovecraft's death at Ladd Observatory and of his birth at his grave site. In July 2013, the Providence City Council designated "H. P. Lovecraft Memorial Square" and installed a commemorative sign at the intersection of Angell and Prospect streets, near the author's former residences.

Appreciation

Within genre

By 1957 Floyd C. Gale of Galaxy Science Fiction said that "like R. E. Howard, Lovecraft seemingly goes on forever; the two decades since their death are as nothing. In any event, they appear more prolific than ever. What with de Camp, Nyberg and Derleth avidly rooting out every scrap of their writings and expanding them into novels, there may never be an end to their posthumous careers". According to Joyce Carol Oates, Lovecraft (and Edgar Allan Poe in the 19th century) has exerted "an incalculable influence on succeeding generations of writers of horror fiction".Horror, fantasy, and science fiction author Stephen King called Lovecraft "the twentieth century's greatest practitioner of the classic horror tale." King has made it clear in his semi-autobiographical non-fiction book Danse Macabre that Lovecraft was responsible for his own fascination with horror and the macabre and was the largest figure to influence his fiction writing.

Literary

Early efforts to revise an established literary view of Lovecraft as an author of 'pulp' were resisted by some eminent critics; in 1945 Edmund Wilson expressed the opinion that "the only real horror in most of these fictions is the horror of bad taste and bad art". But "Mystery and Adventure" columnist Will Cuppy of the New York Herald Tribune recommended to readers a volume of Lovecraft's stories, asserting that "the literature of horror and macabre fantasy belongs with mystery in its broader sense." Gale said that "Lovecraft at his best could build a mood of horror unsurpassed; at his worst, he was laughable". In 1962 Colin Wilson, in his survey of anti-realist trends in fiction The Strength to Dream, cited Lovecraft as one of the pioneers of the "assault on rationality" and included him with M.R. James, H.G. Wells, Aldous Huxley, Tolkien and others as one of the builders of mythicised realities over against the failing project of literary realism. Subsequently Lovecraft began to acquire the status of a cult writer in the counterculture of the 1960s, and reprints of his work proliferated. In 2005 the status of classic American writer conferred by a Library of America edition was accorded to Lovecraft with the publication of Tales, a collection of his weird fiction stories.

Philosophical

Philosopher Graham Harman, seeing Lovecraft as having a unique—though implicit—anti-reductionalist ontology, writes: "No other writer is so perplexed by the gap between objects and the power of language to describe them, or between objects and the qualities they possess." Harman said of leading figures at the initial speculative realism conference (which included philosophers Quentin Meillassoux, Ray Brassier, and Iain Hamilton Grant) that, though they shared no philosophical heroes, all were enthusiastic readers of Lovecraft. Speculative realists, Mark Fisher and other contemporary philosophers, took Lovecraft seriously, mainly because Lovecraft's weird reality as presented in his novels, had nothing to do with the Gothic's insistence in the supernatural, but presented another reality incomprehensible to the human mind, but nonetheless real. According to scholar S. T. Joshi: "There is never an entity in Lovecraft that is not in some fashion material".

Themes

Forbidden knowledge

Forbidden, dark, esoterically veiled knowledge is a central theme in many of Lovecraft's works. Many of his characters are driven by curiosity or scientific endeavor, and in many of his stories the knowledge they uncover proves Promethean in nature, either filling the seeker with regret for what they have learned, destroying them psychologically, or completely destroying the person who holds the knowledge.

Some critics argue that this theme is a reflection of Lovecraft's contempt of the world around him, causing him to search inwardly for knowledge and inspiration.

Non-human influences on humanity

The beings of Lovecraft's mythos often have human servants; Cthulhu, for instance, is worshiped under various names by cults among both the Greenlandic Inuit and voodoo circles of Louisiana, and in many other parts of the world.

These worshippers served a useful narrative purpose for Lovecraft. Many beings of the Mythos were too powerful to be defeated by human opponents, and so horrific that direct knowledge of them meant insanity for the victim. When dealing with such beings, Lovecraft needed a way to provide expositionand build tension without bringing the story to a premature end. Human followers gave him a way to reveal information about their "gods" in a diluted form, and also made it possible for his protagonists to win paltry victories. Lovecraft, like his contemporaries, envisioned "savages" as closer to supernatural knowledge unknown to civilized man.

Inherited guilt

Another recurring theme in Lovecraft's stories is the idea that descendants in a bloodline can never escape the stain of crimes committed by their forebears, at least if the crimes are atrocious enough. Descendants may be very far removed, both in place and in time (and, indeed, in culpability), from the act itself, and yet, they may be haunted by the revenant past, e.g. "The Rats in the Walls", "The Lurking Fear", "Arthur Jermyn", "The Alchemist", The Shadow over Innsmouth, "The Doom that Came to Sarnath" and The Case of Charles Dexter Ward.

Fate

Often in Lovecraft's works the protagonist is not in control of his own actions, or finds it impossible to change course. Many of his characters would be free from danger if they simply managed to run away; however, this possibility either never arises or is somehow curtailed by some outside force, such as in "The Colour Out of Space" and "The Dreams in the Witch House". Often his characters are subject to a compulsive influence from powerful malevolent or indifferent beings. As with the inevitability of one's ancestry, eventually even running away, or death itself, provides no safety ("The Thing on the Doorstep", "The Outsider", The Case of Charles Dexter Ward, etc.). In some cases, this doom is manifest in the entirety of humanity, and no escape is possible (The Shadow Out of Time).

Civilization under threat

Lovecraft was familiar with the work of the German conservative-revolutionary theorist Oswald Spengler, whose pessimistic thesis of the decadence of the modern West formed a crucial element in Lovecraft's overall anti-modern worldview. Spenglerian imagery of cyclical decay is present in particular in At the Mountains of Madness. S. T. Joshi, in H. P. Lovecraft: The Decline of the West, places Spengler at the center of his discussion of Lovecraft's political and philosophical ideas.

Lovecraft wrote to Clark Ashton Smith in 1927: "It is my belief, and was so long before Spengler put his seal of scholarly proof on it, that our mechanical and industrial age is one of frank decadence". Lovecraft was also acquainted with the writings of another German philosopher of decadence: Friedrich Nietzsche.

Lovecraft frequently dealt with the idea of civilization struggling against dark, primitive barbarism. In some stories this struggle is at an individual level; many of his protagonists are cultured, highly educated men who are gradually corrupted by some obscure and feared influence.

In such stories, the curse is often a hereditary one, either because of interbreeding with non-humans (e.g., "Facts Concerning the Late Arthur Jermyn and His Family" (1920), The Shadow over Innsmouth (1931)) or through direct magical influence (The Case of Charles Dexter Ward). Physical and mental degradation often come together; this theme of 'tainted blood' may represent concerns relating to Lovecraft's own family history, particularly the death of his father due to what Lovecraft must have suspected to be a syphilitic disorder.

In other tales, an entire society is threatened by barbarism. Sometimes the barbarism comes as an external threat, with a civilized race destroyed in war (e.g., "Polaris"). Sometimes, an isolated pocket of humanity falls into decadence and atavism of its own accord (e.g., "The Lurking Fear"). But most often, such stories involve a civilized culture being gradually undermined by a malevolent underclass influenced by inhuman forces.

It is likely that the "Roaring Twenties" left Lovecraft disillusioned as he was still obscure and struggling with the basic necessities of daily life, combined with seeing non-Western European immigrants in New York City.

Race, ethnicity, and class

Race is the most controversial aspect of Lovecraft's legacy, expressed in many disparaging remarks against the various non-Anglo-Saxon races and cultures in his work. As he grew older, his original Anglo-Saxon racial worldview softened into a classism or elitism which regarded the superior race to include all those self-ennobled through high culture. From the start, Lovecraft did not hold all white people in uniform high regard, but rather esteemed the English people and those of English descent. He praised non-WASP groups such as Hispanics and Jews; however his private writings on groups such as Irish Catholics, German immigrants and African-Americans were consistently negative. In an early poem, the 1912 On the Creation of Niggers, Lovecraft describes black people not as human but "beasts... in semi-human figure, filled it with vice". In his early published essays, private letters and personal utterances, he argued for a strong color line to preserve race and culture. He made these arguments by direct disparagement of various races in his journalism and letters, and perhaps allegorically in his fiction concerning non-human races. Some have interpreted his racial attitude as being more cultural than brutally biological: Lovecraft showed sympathy to those who adopted Western culture, even to the extent of marrying a Jewish woman whom he viewed as "well assimilated". While Lovecraft's racial attitude has been seen as directly influenced by the society of his day, especially the New England society he grew up in, his racism appeared stronger than the general popular viewpoint.

Risks of a scientific era

At the turn of the 20th century, humanity's increased reliance upon science was both opening new worlds and solidifying understanding of ours. Lovecraft portrays this potential for a growing gap of man's understanding of the universe as a potential for horror, most notably in "The Colour Out of Space", where the inability of science to comprehend a contaminated meteorite leads to horror.

In a letter to James F. Morton in 1923, Lovecraft specifically pointed to Einstein's theory on relativity as throwing the world into chaos and making the cosmos a jest; in a letter to Woodburn Harris in 1929, he speculated that technological comforts risk the collapse of science. Indeed, at a time when men viewed science as limitless and powerful, Lovecraft imagined alternative potential and fearful outcomes. In "The Call of Cthulhu", Lovecraft's characters encounter architecture which is "abnormal, non-Euclidean, and loathsomely redolent of spheres and dimensions apart from ours". Non-Euclidean geometry is the mathematical language and background of Einstein's general theory of relativity, and Lovecraft references it repeatedly in exploring alien archaeology.

Religion

Lovecraft's works are ruled by several distinct pantheons of deities (actually aliens worshiped as such by humans) who are either indifferent or actively hostile to humanity. Lovecraft's actual philosophy has been termed "cosmic indifference" and this is expressed in his fiction. Several of Lovecraft's stories of the Old Ones (alien beings of the Cthulhu Mythos) propose alternate mythic human origins in contrast to those found in the creation stories of existing religions, expanding on a natural world view. For instance, in Lovecraft's At the Mountains of Madness it is proposed that humankind was actually created as a slave race by the Old Ones, and that life on Earth as we know it evolved from scientific experiments abandoned by the Elder Things. Protagonist characters in Lovecraft are usually educated men, citing scientific and rational evidence to support their non-faith. "Herbert West – Reanimator" reflects on the atheism common in academic circles. In "The Silver Key", the character Randolph Carter loses the ability to dream and seeks solace in religion, specifically Congregationalism, but does not find it and ultimately loses faith.

Lovecraft himself adopted the stance of atheism early in life. In 1932, he wrote in a letter to Robert E. Howard:

> All I say is that I think it is damned unlikely that anything like a central cosmic will, a spirit world, or an eternal survival of personality exist. They are the most preposterous and unjustified of all the guesses which can be made about the universe, and I am not enough of a hairsplitter to pretend that I don't regard them as arrant and negligible moonshine. In theory, I am an agnostic, but pending the appearance of radical evidence I must be classed, practically and provisionally, as an atheist.

Superstition

In 1926, famed magician and escapist Harry Houdini asked Lovecraft to ghostwrite a treatise exploring the topic of superstition. Houdini's unexpected death later that year halted the project, but The Cancer of Superstition was partially completed by Lovecraft along with collaborator C. M. Eddy, Jr. A previously unknown manuscript of the work was discovered in 2016 in a collection owned by a magic shop. The book states "all superstitious beliefs are relics of a common 'prehistoric ignorance' in humans," and goes on to explore various superstitious beliefs in different cultures and times."

Influences on Lovecraft

Some of Lovecraft's work was inspired by his own nightmares. His interest started from his childhood days when his grandfather would tell him Gothic horror stories.

Lovecraft's most significant literary influence was Edgar Allan Poe. He had a British writing style due to his love of British literature. Like Lovecraft, Poe's work was out of step with the prevailing literary trends of his era. Both authors created distinctive, singular worlds of fantasy and employed archaisms in their writings. This influence can be found in such works as his novella The Shadow Over Innsmouth where Lovecraft references Poe's story The Imp of the Perverse by name in Chapter 3, and in his poem "Nemesis", where the "... ghoul-guarded gateways of slumber" suggest the "... ghoul-haunted woodland of Weir" found in Poe's "Ulalume". A direct quote from the poem and a reference to Poe's only novel The Narrative of Arthur Gordon Pym of Nantucket is alluded to in Lovecraft's magnum opus At the Mountains of Madness. Both authors shared many biographical similarities as well, such as the loss of their fathers at young ages and an early interest in poetry.

He was influenced by Arthur Machen's carefully constructed tales concerning the survival of ancient evil into modern times in an otherwise realistic world and his beliefs in hidden mysteries which lay behind reality. Lovecraft was also influenced by authors such as Oswald Spengler and Robert W. Chambers. Chambers was the writer of The King in Yellow, of whom Lovecraft wrote in a letter to Clark Ashton Smith: "Chambers is like Rupert Hughes and a few other fallen Titans – equipped with the right brains and education but wholly out of the habit of using them". Lovecraft's discovery of the stories of Lord Dunsany, with their pantheon of mighty gods existing in dreamlike outer realms, moved his writing in a new direction, resulting in a series of imitative fantasies in a "Dreamlands" setting.

Lovecraft also cited Algernon Blackwood as an influence, quoting The Centaur in the head paragraph of "The Call of Cthulhu". He declared Blackwood's story "The Willows" to be the single best piece of weird fiction ever written.

Another inspiration came from a completely different source: scientific progress in biology, astronomy, geology, and physics. His study of science contributed to Lovecraft's view of the human race as insignificant, powerless, and doomed in a materialistic and mechanistic universe. Lovecraft was a keen amateur astronomer from his youth, often visiting the Ladd Observatory in Providence, and penning numerous astronomical articles for local newspapers. His astronomical telescope is now housed in the rooms of the August Derleth Society.

Lovecraft's materialist views led him to espouse his philosophical views through his fiction; these philosophical views came to be called cosmicism. Cosmicism took on a dark tone with his creation of what is today often called the Cthulhu Mythos, a pantheon of alien extra-dimensional deities and horrors which predate humanity, and which are hinted at in eons-old myths and legends. The term "Cthulhu Mythos" was coined by Lovecraft's correspondent and fellow author, August Derleth, after Lovecraft's death; Lovecraft jocularly referred to his artificial mythology as "Yog-Sothothery".

Lovecraft considered himself a man best suited to the early 18th century. His writing style, especially in his many letters, owes much to Augustan British writers of the Enlightenment like Joseph Addison and Jonathan Swift.

Among the books found in his library (as evidenced in Lovecraft's Library by S. T. Joshi) was The Seven Who Were Hanged by Leonid Andreyev and A Strange Manuscript Found in a Copper Cylinder by James De Mille.

Lovecraft's style has often been subject to criticism, yet scholars such as S. T. Joshi have shown that Lovecraft consciously utilized a variety of literary devices to form a unique style of his own – these include conscious archaism, prose-poetic techniques combined with essay-form techniques, alliteration, anaphora, crescendo, transferred epithet, metaphor, symbolism, and colloquialism.

Influence on culture

Lovecraft was relatively unknown during his own time. While his stories appeared in the pages of prominent pulp magazines such as Weird Tales (eliciting letters of outrage as often as letters of praise from regular readers), not many people knew his name. He did, however, correspond regularly with other contemporary writers such as Clark Ashton Smith and August Derleth, who became good friends of his, even though they never met in person. This group of writers became known as the "Lovecraft Circle", since their writing freely borrowed elements of Lovecraft's stories, with his encouragement: the mysterious books with disturbing names, the pantheon of ancient alien entities such as Cthulhu and Azathoth, and eldritch places such as the New England town of Arkham and its Miskatonic University.

After Lovecraft's death, the Lovecraft Circle carried on. August Derleth in particular added to and expanded on Lovecraft's vision, not without controversy. While Lovecraft considered his pantheon of alien gods a mere plot device, Derleth created an entire cosmology, complete with a war between the good Elder Gods and the evil Outer Gods, such as Cthulhu and his ilk. The forces of good were supposed to have won, locking Cthulhu and others up beneath the earth, in the ocean, and so forth. Derleth's Cthulhu Mythos stories went on to associate different gods with the traditional four elements of fire, air, earth and water — an artificial constraint which required rationalizations on Derleth's part as Lovecraft himself never envisioned such a scheme.

Lovecraft's fiction has been grouped into three categories by some critics. While Lovecraft did not refer to these categories himself, he did once write: "There are my 'Poe' pieces and my 'Dunsany pieces' — but alas — where are any Lovecraft pieces?"

- Macabre stories (c. 1905–1920);

- Dream Cycle stories (c. 1920–1927);

- Cthulhu / Lovecraft Mythos stories (c. 1925–1935).

Lovecraft's writing, particularly the so-called Cthulhu Mythos, has influenced fiction authors including modern horror and fantasy writers. Stephen King, Ramsey Campbell, Bentley Little, Joe R. Lansdale, Alan Moore, Junji Ito, F. Paul Wilson, Brian Lumley, Caitlín R. Kiernan, William S. Burroughs, and Neil Gaiman, have cited Lovecraft as one of their primary influences. Beyond direct adaptation, Lovecraft and his stories have had a profound impact on popular culture. Some influence was direct, as he was a friend, inspiration, and correspondent to many of his contemporaries, such as August Derleth, Robert E. Howard, Robert Bloch and Fritz Leiber. Many later figures were influenced by Lovecraft's works, including author and artist Clive Barker, prolific horror writer Stephen King, Brian Keene has several novels based on the Old Gods, comics writers Alan Moore, Neil Gaiman and Mike Mignola, English author Colin Wilson, film directors John Carpenter, Stuart Gordon, Guillermo Del Toro and artist H. R. Giger. Japan has also been significantly inspired and terrified by Lovecraft's creations and thus even entered the manga and anime media. Chiaki J. Konaka is an acknowledged disciple and has participated in Cthulhu Mythos, expanding several Japanese versions. He is an anime scriptwriter who tends to add elements of cosmicism, and is credited for spreading the influence of Lovecraft among anime base. Along with Junji Ito, other influential manga artists have also been inspired by Lovecraft. Novelist and manga author, Hideyuki Kikuchi, incorporated a number of locations, beings and events from the works of Lovecraft into the manga Taimashin.

Argentine writer Jorge Luis Borges wrote his short story "There Are More Things" in memory of Lovecraft. Contemporary French writer Michel Houellebecq wrote a literary biography of Lovecraft called H. P. Lovecraft: Against the World, Against Life. Prolific American writer Joyce Carol Oates wrote an introduction for a collection of Lovecraft stories. The Library of America published a volume of Lovecraft's work in 2005, a reversal of traditional judgment that "has been nothing so far from the accepted canon as Lovecraft". French philosophers Gilles Deleuze and Félix Guattari refer to Lovecraft in A Thousand Plateaus, calling the short story "Through the Gates of the Silver Key" one of his masterpieces.

Music

Lovecraft's fictional Mythos has influenced a number of musicians.

- The psychedelic rock band H. P. Lovecraft (who shortened their name to Lovecraft and then Love Craft in the 1970s) released the albums H. P. Lovecraft and H. P. Lovecraft II in 1967 and 1968 respectively; their titles included "The White Ship" and "At the Mountains of Madness", both titled after Lovecraft stories. The founders of their record company, Bill Traut and George Badonsky, were fans of the author and gained August Derleth's permission to use Lovecraft's name for the band.

- Metallica recorded a song inspired by "The Call of Cthulhu", an instrumental titled "The Call of Ktulu", and another song based on The Shadow Over Innsmouth titled "The Thing That Should Not Be", and another based on Frank Belknap Long's "The Hounds of Tindalos", titled "All Nightmare Long". Later, they released the song Dream No More, which mentions the awakening of Cthulhu.

- The Darkest of the Hillside Thickets' entire repertoire is Lovecraft-based.

- German metal group Mekong Delta made an album called The Music of Erich Zann.

- "You're So Dark", B-side from AM's "One For The Road", by Arctic Monkeys, mentions Lovecraft as one of the authors of the "dark" culture along with Edgar Allan Poe.

- Heavy metal band Mercyful Fate produced "The Mad Arab (Part 1)" and "Kutulu (The Mad Arab Part 2)" on their albums Time and Into The Unknown based on Abdul Alhazred, the "Mad Arab" who created the Necronomicon in the Lovecraft universe.

- "Lovecraft in Brooklyn" is the eighth track on the Mountain Goats' 2000 album Heretic Pride.

- Deathrock band Rudimentary Peni's Cacophony (album) from 1988 was inspired by Lovecraft's work, as many of the song titles and lyrics are derived from his writing. Lead vocalist and guitarist Nick Blinko has cited his fascination with the Lovecraft mythos is what influenced him to create the album.

- Cradle of Filth's song Mother of Abominations begins with the chant, "Ia Ia Chtulhu Ftagn"

Games

Lovecraft has also influenced gaming, despite having hated games during his lifetime. Chaosium's tabletop role-playing game Call of Cthulhu, released in 1981 and currently in its seventh major edition, was one of the first games to draw heavily from Lovecraft. Novel to the game was the Lovecraft inspired insanity mechanic, which allowed for player characters to go insane from contact with cosmic horrors. This mechanic would go on to make appearance in subsequent table top and video games. 1987 saw the release of one of the first Lovecraftian board games, Arkham Horror, which sold extremely well. Though few subsequent Lovecraftian board games were released annually between 1987 and 2014, the years after 2014 saw a surge in the number of Lovecraftian board games, possibly because of the entry of Lovecraft's work into the public domaincombined with a revival of interest in board games.

Few video games are direct adaptations of Lovecraft's works, but many video games have been inspired or heavily influenced by Lovecraft. Horror games especially can incorporate Cthulthean terrors, despite the conflict between "act-and-prevail" nature of video games and the cosmic hopelessness of Lovecraftian horror. Besides employing Cthulthean antagonists, games that invoke Lovecraftian horror have used mechanics such as insanity effects, or even fourth wall breaking effects that suggest to players that something has gone wrong with their game consoles.

Lovecraft as a character in fiction

Aside from his thinly veiled appearance in Robert Bloch's "The Shambler from the Stars", Lovecraft continues to be used as a character in supernatural fiction. An early version of Ray Bradbury's "The Exiles" uses Lovecraft as a character, who makes a brief, 600-word appearance eating ice cream in front of a fire and complaining about how cold he is. Lovecraft and some associates are included at length in Robert Anton Wilsonand Robert Shea's The Illuminatus! Trilogy (1975). Lovecraft makes an appearance as a rotting corpse in The Chinatown Death Cloud Peril by Paul Malmont, a novel with fictionalized versions of a number of period writers. John Shirley's story When Death Wakes Me To Myself offers a tale of a therapy patient slowly remembering a former incarnation when he was H.P. Lovecraft.

Other notable works with Lovecraft as a character include Richard Lupoff's Lovecraft's Book (1985), Cast a Deadly Spell (1991), H.P. Lovecraft's: Necronomicon (1993), Witch Hunt (1994), Out of Mind: The Stories of H. P. Lovecraft (1998), Stargate SG-1: Roswell (2007), and Alan Moore's comic Providence (2015–17). Lovecraft also appears in the Season 6, Episode 21 episode "Let it Bleed" of the TV show Supernatural. A satirical version of Lovecraft named "H. P. Hatecraft" appeared as a recurring character on the Cartoon Network television series Scooby-Doo! Mystery Incorporated. A character based on Lovecraft also appears in the visual novel Shikkoku no Sharnoth: What a Beautiful Tomorrow, under the name "Howard Phillips" (or "Mr. Howard" to most of the main characters). Another character based on Lovecraft appears in Afterlife with Archie. He appears as a minor character in Brian Clevinger's comic book series Atomic Robo, as an acquaintance and fellow-scientist of Nikola Tesla, having been driven insane by his involvement in the Tunguska Event which exposed him to the hidden horrors of the wider universe. He is eventually killed when his body becomes host to an extradimensional being infecting the timestream. Lovecraft is a central plot element, as well as a character in Paul La Farge's 2017 novel, The Night Ocean. In the Japanese manga and anime Bungo Stray Dogs there is a character known as Howard Phillips Lovecraft who, like other characters in the series, is named after great literates. Even his power, "The Great Old Ones" pays homage to his classic book, The Call of Cthulhu, which grants him the ability of transforming himself into an octopus like monster resembling Cthulhu.

The short story "The Invention of H. P. Lovecraft" by S. K. Azoulay suggests that Lovecraft was a fictional creation invented by Jorge Luis Borges.

Editions and collections of Lovecraft's work

For most of the 20th century, the definitive editions (specifically At the Mountains of Madness and Other Novels, Dagon and Other Macabre Tales, The Dunwich Horror and Others, and The Horror in the Museum and Other Revisions) of his prose fiction were published by Arkham House, a publisher originally started with the intent of publishing the work of Lovecraft, but which has since published a considerable amount of other literature as well. Penguin Classics has at present issued three volumes of Lovecraft's works: The Call of Cthulhu and Other Weird Stories, The Thing on the Doorstep and Other Weird Stories, and most recently The Dreams in the Witch House and Other Weird Stories. They collect the standard texts as edited by S. T. Joshi, most of which were available in the Arkham House editions, with the exception of the restored text of "The Shadow Out of Time" from The Dreams in the Witch House, which had been previously released by small-press publisher Hippocampus Press. In 2005 the prestigious Library of America canonized Lovecraft with a volume of his stories edited by Peter Straub, and Random House's Modern Library line have issued the "definitive edition" of Lovecraft's At the Mountains of Madness (also including "Supernatural Horror in Literature").

Lovecraft's poetry is collected in The Ancient Track: The Complete Poetical Works of H. P. Lovecraft (Night Shade Books, 2001), while much of his juvenilia, various essays on philosophical, political and literary topics, antiquarian travelogues, and other things, can be found in Miscellaneous Writings (Arkham House, 1989). Lovecraft's essay "Supernatural Horror in Literature", first published in 1927, is a historical survey of horror literature available with endnotes as The Annotated Supernatural Horror in Literature.

Letters

Although Lovecraft is known mostly for his works of weird fiction, the bulk of his writing consists of voluminous letters about a variety of topics, from weird fiction and art criticism to politics and history. Lovecraft's biographer L. Sprague de Camp estimates that Lovecraft wrote 100,000 letters in his lifetime, a fifth of which are believed to survive.

He sometimes dated his letters 200 years before the current date, which would have put the writing back in US colonial times, before the American Revolution (a war that offended his Anglophilia). He explained that he thought that the 18th and 20th centuries were the "best", the former being a period of noble grace, and the latter a century of science.

Lovecraft was not an active letter-writer in youth. In 1931 he admitted: "In youth I scarcely did any letter-writing — thanking anybody for a present was so much of an ordeal that I would rather have written a two hundred fifty-line pastoral or a twenty-page treatise on the rings of Saturn." (SL 3.369–70). The initial interest in letters stemmed from his correspondence with his cousin Phillips Gamwell but even more important was his involvement in the amateur journalism movement, which was initially responsible for the enormous number of letters Lovecraft produced.

Despite his light letter-writing in youth, in later life his correspondence was so voluminous that it has been estimated that he may have written around 30,000 letters to various correspondents, a figure which places him second only to Voltaire as an epistolarian. Lovecraft's later correspondence is primarily to fellow weird fiction writers, rather than to the amateur journalist friends of his earlier years.

Lovecraft clearly states that his contact to numerous different people through letter-writing was one of the main factors in broadening his view of the world: "I found myself opened up to dozens of points of view which would otherwise never have occurred to me. My understanding and sympathies were enlarged, and many of my social, political, and economic views were modified as a consequence of increased knowledge." (SL 4.389).

Today there are five publishing houses that have released letters from Lovecraft, most prominently Arkham House with its five-volume edition Selected Letters (these volumes severely abridge the letters they contain). Other publishers are Hippocampus Press (Letters to Alfred Galpin et al.), Night Shade Books (Mysteries of Time and Spirit: The Letters of H. P. Lovecraft and Donald Wandrei et al.), Necronomicon Press (Letters to Samuel Loveman and Vincent Starrett et al.), and University of Tampa Press (O Fortunate Floridian: H. P. Lovecraft's Letters to R. H. Barlow). S.T. Joshi is supervising an ongoing series of volumes collecting Lovecraft's unabridged letters to particular correspondents.

Lord of a Visible World: An Autobiography in Letters was published in 2000, in which Lovecraft's letters are arranged according to themes, such as adolescence and travel.

Copyright

Despite several claims to the contrary, there is currently no evidence that any company or individual owns the copyright to any of Lovecraft's work, and it is generally accepted that it has passed into the public domain.

There has been controversy over the copyright status of many of Lovecraft's works, especially his later works. Lovecraft had specified that the young R. H. Barlow would serve as executor of his literary estate, but these instructions had not been incorporated into his will. Nevertheless his surviving aunt carried out his expressed wishes, and Barlow was given charge of the massive and complex literary estate upon Lovecraft's death.

Barlow deposited the bulk of the papers, including the voluminous correspondence, with the John Hay Library, and attempted to organize and maintain Lovecraft's other writing. August Derleth, an older and more established writer than Barlow, vied for control of the literary estate. One result of these conflicts was the legal confusion over who owned what copyrights.

All works published before 1923 are public domain in the US. With respect to works published later, ownership of the copyrights is disputed. Before the United States Copyright Act of 1976, copyright lasted for 28 years from publication and a work that did not have its copyright renewed passed into the public domain. The Copyright Act of 1976 retroactively extended this renewal period for all works to a period of 47 years and the Sonny Bono Copyright Term Extension Act of 1998 added another 20 years to that, for a total of 95 years from publication. But everything turned on the renewal or expiration of copyright at the end of the first 28-year term.

The European Union Copyright Duration Directive of 1993 extended the copyrights to 70 years after the author's death. All of Lovecraft's works published during his lifetime became public domain in all 27 European Union countries on January 1, 2008. In those Berne Convention countries that have implemented only the minimum copyright period, copyright expires 50 years after the author's death.

Lovecraft protégés and part owners of Arkham House, August Derleth and Donald Wandrei, often claimed copyrights over Lovecraft's works. On October 9, 1947, Derleth purchased all rights to Weird Tales. However, since April 1926 at the latest, Lovecraft had reserved to himself all second printing rights to stories published in Weird Tales. Weird Tales may only have owned the rights to at most six of Lovecraft's tales. Again, even if Derleth did obtain the copyrights to Lovecraft's tales, there is no evidence that the copyrights were renewed. Following Derleth's death in 1971, his attorney proclaimed that all of Lovecraft's literary material was part of the Derleth estate and that it would be "protected to the fullest extent possible."

S. T. Joshi concludes in his biography of Lovecraft that Derleth's claims are "almost certainly fictitious" and that most of Lovecraft's works published in the amateur press are most likely now in the public domain. The copyright for Lovecraft's works would have been inherited by the only surviving heir named in his 1912 will, his aunt Annie Gamwell. When Gamwell died in 1941, the copyrights passed to her remaining descendants, Ethel Phillips Morrish and Edna Lewis, who then signed a document, sometimes referred to as the Morrish-Lewis gift, permitting Arkham House to republish Lovecraft's works while retaining the copyrights for themselves. Searches of the Library of Congress have failed to find any evidence that these copyrights were renewed after the 28-year period, making it likely that these works are now in the public domain.

Chaosium, publishers of the Call of Cthulhu role-playing game, have a trademark on the phrase "The Call of Cthulhu" for use in game products. TSR, Inc., original publisher of the Advanced Dungeons & Dragons role-playing game, included a section on the Cthulhu Mythos in one of the game's earlier supplements, Deities & Demigods (originally published in 1980 and later renamed to "Legends & Lore"). TSR later agreed to remove this section at Chaosium's request.

In 2009, Lovecraft Holdings, LLC, a company based out of Providence, filed trademark claims for clothing graphics of Lovecraft's name and silhouette.

Regardless of the legal disagreements surrounding Lovecraft's works, Lovecraft himself was extremely generous with his own works and encouraged others to borrow ideas from his stories and build on them, particularly with regard to his Cthulhu Mythos. He encouraged other writers to reference his creations, such as the Necronomicon, Cthulhu and Yog-Sothoth. After his death, many writers have contributed stories and enriched the shared mythology of the Cthulhu Mythos, as well as making numerous references to his work.

World Fantasy Award and H. P. Lovecraft controversy

In 1984, writer Donald Wandrei caused some controversy after he was offered a World Fantasy Award for Life Achievement but refused to accept it because the award was a bust of H. P. Lovecraft that he felt looked more like a caricature of Lovecraft than an actual representation.

In August 2014, author Daniel José Older started a petition to change the World Fantasy Award statuette from a bust of Lovecraft to one of African-American author Octavia Butler. Kevin J. Maroney, editor of The New York Review of Science Fiction, also supported the call for the WFA to be changed from Lovecraft's face, suggesting it be replaced with a symbol representing the fantasy genre. Maroney argued this should be done "not out of disrespect for Lovecraft as a writer or as a central figure in fantasy, but as a courtesy to generations of writers whom the WFA hopes to honor." In response to the campaign, the board of the World Fantasy Awards announced in September 2014 that it was "in discussion" about the future of the award statuette, and in November 2015 it was announced that the World Fantasy Award trophy would no longer be modeled on H. P. Lovecraft.

Locations featured in Lovecraft stories

Lovecraft drew extensively from his native New England for settings in his fiction. Numerous real historical locations are mentioned, and several fictional New England locations make frequent appearances.

Bibliography

Fiction

Title	Date written	Date published	Form
The Tomb	juin-17	mars-22	Short story
Dagon	juil-17	nov-19	Short story
A Reminiscence of Dr. Samuel Johnson	Sum-early Fall 1917	sept-17	Short story
Polaris	Spr-Sum 1918	Dec 1920	Short story
Beyond the Wall of Sleep	Spr 1919	oct-19	Short story
Memory	Spr 1919	May 1923	Flash fiction
Old Bugs	c.Jul 1919	1959	Short Story
The Transition of Juan Romero	16 September 1919	1944	Short story
The White Ship	c.Oct 1919	nov-19	Short story
The Doom that Came to Sarnath	3 December 1919	juin-20	Short story
The Statement of Randolph Carter	Dec 1919	May 1920	Short story
The Street	late 1919	Dec 1920	Short story
The Terrible Old Man	28 January 1920	juil-21	Short story
The Cats of Ulthar	15 June 1920	nov-20	Short story
The Tree	Jan-Jun 1920	oct-21	Short story
Celephaïs	early Nov 1920	May 1922	Short story
From Beyond	16 November 1920	juin-34	Short story
The Temple	c. Jun-Nov 1920	sept-25	Short story
Nyarlathotep	c.Nov 1920	nov-20	Short story
The Picture in the House	12 December 1920	Sum 1921	Short story
Facts Concerning the Late Arthur Jermyn and His Family	Fall 1920	Mar & Jun 1921 as "The White Ape"	Short story
The Nameless City	janv-21	nov-21	Short story
The Quest of Iranon	28 February 1921	Jul-Aug 1935	Short story
The Moon-Bog	March 10, 1921	juin-26	Short Story
Ex Oblivione	1920 – Mar 1921 (unclear)	mars-21	Short story
The Other Gods	14 August 1921	nov-33	Short story
The Outsider	Spr-Sum 1921	Apr 1926	Short story
The Music of Erich Zann	Dec 1921	mars-22	Short story
Sweet Ermengarde	c. 1919–21?	1943	Short story
Hypnos	mars-22	May 1923	Short story
What the Moon Brings	5 June 1922	May 1923	Short story
Azathoth	Fragment Jun 1922	juin-38	Novel fragment
Herbert West–Reanimator	Oct 1921 – Jun 1922	Feb-Jul 1922	Novelette
The Hound	oct-22	Feb 1924	Short story
The Lurking Fear	nov-22	Jan-Apr 1923	Short story
The Rats in the Walls	Aug-Sep 1923	mars-24	Short story

The Unnamable	sept-23	juil-25	Short story
The Festival	oct-23	janv-25	Short story
The Shunned House	oct-24	oct-37	Short story
The Horror at Red Hook	1-2 Aug 1925	janv-27	Short story
He	11 August 1925	sept-26	Short story
In the Vault	18 September 1925	nov-25	Short story
Cool Air	Feb 1926	mars-28	Short story
The Call of Cthulhu	Aug-Sep 1926	Feb 1928	Short story
Pickman's Model	sept-26	oct-27	Short story
The Strange High House in the Mist	9 November 1926	oct-31	Short story
The Silver Key	nov-26	janv-29	Short story
The Dream-Quest of Unknown Kadath	Oct 1926-22 Jan 1927	1943	Novella
The Case of Charles Dexter Ward	Jan-Mar 1, 1927	May & Jul 1941	Novel
The Colour Out of Space	mars-27	sept-27	Short story
The Descendant	Fragment early 1927	1938	Short story fragment
The Very Old Folk	3 November 1927	Sum 1940	Letter excerpt
History of the Necronomicon	sketch Fall 1927	1938	Brief pseudo-history
The Dunwich Horror	Aug 1928	Apr 1929	Short story
Ibid	Sum 1928	janv-38	Short story
The Whisperer in Darkness	24 Feb-Sep 26, 1930	Aug 1931	Novella
At the Mountains of Madness	24 Feb-Mar 22, 1931	Feb-Apr 1936	Novella
The Shadow Over Innsmouth	Nov-Dec 1931	Apr 1936	Novella
The Dreams in the Witch House	Feb 1932	juil-33	Short story
The Thing on the Doorstep	21-24 Aug 1933	janv-37	Short story
The Book	Fragment c.Oct 1933	1938	Short story fragment
The Evil Clergyman	Letter extract Fall 1933	Apr 1939	Letter excerpt
The Shadow Out of Time	10 Nov 1934- February 22, 1935	juin-36	Novella
The Haunter of the Dark	5-9 Nov 1935	Dec 1936	Short story

Collaborations, revisions, and ghost writing

Title	Date written	Date published	Collaborators (or Revision Client)
The Battle that Ended the Century	12571	12571	R. H. Barlow
Bothon	1946	1946	Henry S. Whitehead
The Challenge from Beyond	Aug 1935	13028	C.L. Moore, A. Merritt Robert E. Howard and Frank Belknap Long
Collapsing Cosmoses	1938	1938	R. H. Barlow
The Crawling Chaos	c. Dec 1920	Apr 1921	Winifred V. Jackson
The Curse of Yig	Spring 1928	10898	Zealia Bishop
The Diary of Alonzo Typer	13058	Feb 1938	William Lumley
The Disinterment	13028	13516	Duane W. Rimel
The Electric Executioner	10775	Aug 1930	Adolphe de Castro
The Green Meadow	c. 1918-1919	Spring 1927	Winifred V. Jackson
Four O'Clock	1922	1922	Sonia Greene
The Hoard of the Wizard-Beast	1933	1933	R. H. Barlow
The Horror at Martin's Beach	8188	8706	Sonia Greene
The Horror in the Burying-Ground	c. 1933-1934	May 1937	Hazel Heald
The Horror in the Museum	11963	12236	Hazel Heald
Imprisoned with the Pharaohs	Feb 1924	May-Jul 1924	Harry Houdini
The Last Test	c. Oct-Nov 1927	10533	Adolphe de Castro
The Man of Stone	Summer 1932	11963	Hazel Heald
Medusa's Coil	c. May-Aug 1930	14246	Zealia Bishop
The Mound	c. Dec 1929 – Jan 1930	14916	Zealia Bishop
The Night Ocean	Summer 1936	Winter 1939	R. H. Barlow
Out of the Aeons	c. Aug 1933	Apr 1935	Hazel Heald
Poetry and the Gods	c. Summer 1920	7550	Anna Helen Crofts
The Slaying of the Monster	1933	1933	R. H. Barlow
The Sorcery of Aphlar	1934	1934	Duane W. Rimel
The Thing in the Moonlight	10167	14977	J. Chapman Miske
Through the Gates of the Silver Key	Oct 1932 – Apr 1933	12601	Edgar Hoffmann Price
Till A'the Seas	12785	Summer 1935	R. H. Barlow
The Trap	c. Summer 1931	11749	Henry S. Whitehead
The Tree on the Hill	May 1934	14855	Duane W. Rimel
Two Black Bottles	Jun-oct 1926	Aug 1927	Wilfred Blanch Talman
In the Walls of Eryx	13150	14519	Kenneth Sterling
Winged Death	c. Summer 1932	12479	Hazel Heald
Satan's Servants	1935	1949	Robert Bloch

Great Ghost Stories	1998	1998	Peter Glassman and Barry Moser

Works by August Derleth related to H. P. Lovecraft's works and notes

- The Ancestor
- The Dark Brotherhood
- The Fisherman of Falcon Point
- The Gable Window
- The Horror from the Middle Span
- Innsmouth Clay
- The Lamp of Alhazred
- The Lurker at the Threshold
- The Peabody Heritage
- The Shadow in the Attic
- The Shadow Out of Space
- The Shuttered Room
- The Survivor
- The Watchers Out of Time
- Wentworth's Day
- Witches' Hollow

Unknown authorship

- The Inevitable Conflict. This was published in Amazing Stories (December 1930 and January 1931) under the name P. H. Lovering. A variety of evidence, including statistical analysis of the writing structure, has been put forward to suggest that Lovecraft was not the author.

Juvenilia

- "The Alchemist" (1908 / November 1916)
- "The Beast in the Cave" (Spr 1904–21 Apr 1905 / June 1918)
- "The Haunted House" (<1902; unpublished, nonextant)
- "John, the Detective" (<1902; unpublished, nonextant)
- "The Little Glass Bottle" (c. 1898–9 / 1959)
- "The Mysterious Ship" (1902 / 1959)
- "The Mystery of the Grave-Yard" (c. 1898–9 / 1959)
- "The Noble Eavesdropper" (1897; unpublished, nonextant)
- "The Picture" (1907; unpublished, nonextant)
- "The Secret of the Grave" (<1902; unpublished, nonextant, may simply be "The Mystery of the Grave-Yard")
- "The Secret Cave, or John Lees Adventure" (c. 1898–9 / 1959)

Poetry

- The Poem of Ulysses, or The Odyssey [November 8, 1897]
- Ovid's Metamorphoses [1898–1902]
- H. Lovecraft's Attempted Journey betwixt Providence & Fall River on the N.Y.N.H. & H.R.R. [1901]
- Poemata Minora, Volume II [1902]
  - Ode to Selene or Diana
  - To the Old Pagan Religion
  - On the Ruin of Rome
  - To Pan
  - On the Vanity of Human Ambition
- C.S.A. 1861-1865: To the Starry Cross of the SOUTH [1902]
- De Triumpho Naturae [July 1905]
- The Members of the Men's Club of the First Universalist Church of Providence, R.I., to Its President, About to Leave for Florida on Account of His Health [c. 1908–12]
- To His Mother on Thanksgiving [November 30, 1911]
- To Mr. Terhune, on His Historical Fiction [c. 1911–13]
- Providence in 2000 A.D. [March 4, 1912]
- New-England Fallen [April 1912]
- On the Creation of Niggers [1912]
- Fragment on Whitman [c. 1912]
- On Robert Browning [c. 1912]
- On a New-England Village Seen by Moonlight [September 7, 1913]
- Quinsnicket Park [1913]
- To Mr. Munroe, on His Instructive and Entertaining Account of Switzerland [January 1, 1914]
- Ad Criticos [January–May? 1914]
- Frusta Praemunitus [June? 1914]
- De Scriptore Mulieroso [June? 1914]
- To General Villa [Summer 1914]
- On a Modern Lothario [July–August 1914]
- The End of the Jackson War [October 1914]
- To the Members of the Pin-Feathers on the Merits of Their Organisation, and of Their New Publication, The Pinfeather [November 1914]

- To the Rev. James Pyke [November 1914]

- To an Accomplished Young Gentlewoman on Her Birthday, Decr. 2, 1914 [December 2? 1914]

- Regner Lodbrog's Epicedium [c. December 1914]

- The Power of Wine: A Satire [c. December 8, 1914]

- The Teuton's Battle-Song [c. December 17, 1914]

- New England [December 18, 1914]

- Gryphus in Asinum Mutatus [1914?]

- To the Members of the United Amateur Press Association from the Providence Amateur Press Club [c. January 1, 1915]

- March [March 1915]

- 1914 [March 1915]

- The Simple Speller's Tale [April 1915]

- On Slang [April 1915]

- An Elegy on Franklin Chase Clark, M.D. [April 29, 1915]

- The Bay-Stater's Policy [June 1915]

- The Crime of Crimes [July 1915]

- Ye Ballade of Patrick von Flynn [c. August 23, 1915]

- The Issacsonio-Mortoniad [c. September 14, 1915]

- On Receiving a Picture of Swans [c. September 14, 1915]

- Unda; or, The Bride of the Sea [c. September 30, 1915]

- On "Unda; or, The Bride of the Sea" [c. September 30, 1915]

- To Charlie of the Comics [c. September 30, 1915]

- Gems from in a Minor Key [October 1915]

- The State of Poetry [October 1915]

- The Magazine Poet [October 1915]

- A Mississippi Autumn [December 1915]

- On the Cowboys of the West [December 1915]

- To Samuel Loveman, Esquire, on His Poetry and Drama, Written in the Elizabethan Style [December 1915]

- An American to Mother England [January 1916]

- The Bookstall [January 1916]

- A Rural Summer Eve [January 1916]

- To the Late John H. Fowler, Esq. [March 1916]

- R. Kleiner, Laureatus, in Heliconem [April 1916]

- Temperance Song [Spring 1916]

- Lines on Gen. Robert Edward Lee [c. May 18, 1916]
- Content [June 1916]
- My Lost Love [c. June 10, 1916]
- The Beauties of Peace [June 27, 1916]
- The Smile [July 1916]
- Epitaph on ye Letterr Rrr........ [August 29, 1916]
- The Dead Bookworm [c. August 29, 1916]
- On Phillips Gamwell [September 1, 1916]
- Inspiration [October 1916]
- Respite [October 1916]
- The Rose of England [October 1916]
- The Unknown [October 1916]
- Ad Balneum [c. October 1916]
- On Kelso the Poet [October? 1916]
- Providence Amateur Press Club (Deceased) to the Athenaeum Club of Journalism [November 24, 1916]
- Brotherhood [December 1916]
- Brumalia [December 1916]
- The Poe-et's Nightmare [1916]
- Futurist Art [January 1917]
- On Receiving a Picture of the Marshes of Ipswich [January 1917]
- The Rutted Road [January 1917]
- An Elegy on Phillips Gamwell, Esq. [January 5, 1917]
- Lines on Graduation from the R.I. Hospital's School of Nurses [c. January 13, 1917]
- Fact and Fancy [February 1917]
- The Nymph's Reply to the Modern Business Man [February 1917]
- Pacifist War Song—1917 [March 1917]
- Percival Lowell [March 1917]
- To Mr. Lockhart, on His Poetry [March 1917]
- Britannia Victura [April 1917]
- Spring [April 1917]
- A Garden [April 1917]
- Sonnet on Myself [April 1917]
- April [April 24, 1917]
- Iterum Conjunctae [May 1917]

- The Peace Advocate [May 1917]

- To Greece, 1917 [May? 1917]

- On Receiving a Picture of ye Towne of Templeton, in the Colonie of Massachusetts-Bay, with Mount Monadnock, in New-Hampshire, Shown in the Distance [June 1917]

- The Poet of Passion [June 1917]

- Earth and Sky [July 1917]

- Ode for July Fourth, 1917 [July 1917]

- On the Death of a Rhyming Critic [July 1917]

- Prologue to "Fragments from an Hour of Inspiration" by Jonathan E. Hoag [July 1917]

- To M.W.M. [July 1917]

- To the Incomparable Clorinda [July 1917]

- To Saccharissa, Fairest of Her Sex [July 1917]

- To Rhodoclia—Peerless among Maidens [July 1917]

- To Belinda, Favourite of the Graces [July 1917]

- To Heliodora—Sister of Cytheraea [July 1917]

- To Mistress Sophia Simple, Queen of the Cinema [August 1917]

- An American to the British Flag [November 1917]

- Autumn [November 1917]

- Nemesis [November 1, 1917]

- Astrophobos [c. November 25, 1917]

- Lines on the 25th. Anniversary of the Providence Evening News, 1892-1917 [December 1917]

- Sunset [December 1917]

- Old Christmas [late 1917]

- To the Arcadian [late 1917]

- To the Nurses of the Red Cross [1917]

- The Introduction [1917?]

- A Summer Sunset and Evening [1917?]

- A Winter Wish [January 2, 1918]

- Laeta; a Lament [February 1918]

- To Jonathan E. Hoag, Esq. [February 1918]

- The Volunteer [February 1918]

- Ad Britannos—1918 [April 1918]

- Ver Rusticum [April 1, 1918]

- To Mr. Kleiner, on Receiving from Him the Poetical Works of Addison, Gay, and Somerville [April 10, 1918]

- A Pastoral Tragedy of Appleton, Wisconsin [c. May 27, 1918]
- On a Battlefield in Picardy [May 30, 1918]
- Psychopompos: A Tale in Rhyme [late 1917-summer 1918]
- A June Afternoon [June 1918]
- The Spirit of Summer [June 27, 1918]
- Grace [July 1918]
- The Link [July 1918]
- To Alan Seeger [July 1918]
- August [August 1918]
- Damon and Delia, a Pastoral [August 1918]
- Phaeton [August 1918]
- To Arthur Goodenough, Esq. [August 20, 1918]
- Hellas [September 1918]
- To Delia, Avoiding Damon [September 1918]
- Alfredo; a Tragedy [September 14, 1918]
- The Eidolon [October 1918]
- Monos: An Ode [October 1918]
- Germania—1918 [November 1918]
- To Col. Linkaby Didd [November 1, 1918]
- Ambition [December 1918]
- A Cycle of Verse [November–December 1918]
  - Oceanus
  - Clouds
  - Mother Earth
- To the Eighth of November [December 13, 1918]
- To the A.H.S.P.C., on Receipt of the Christmas Pippin [December? 1918]
- The Conscript [1918?]
- Greetings [January 1919]
- Theodore Roosevelt [January 1919]
- To Maj.-Gen. Omar Bundy, U.S.A. [January 1919]
- To Jonathan Hoag, Esq. [February 1919]
- Despair [c. February 19, 1919]
- In Memoriam: J.E.T.D. [March 1919]
- Revelation [March 1919]
- April Dawn [April 10, 1919]

- Amissa Minerva [May 1919]
- Damon: A Monody [May 1919]
- Hylas and Myrrha: A Tale [May 1919]
- North and South Britons [May 1919]
- To the A.H.S.P.C., on Receipt of the May Pippin [May? 1919]
- Helene Hoffman Cole: 1893-1919 [June 1919]
- John Oldham: A Defence [June 1919]
- On Prohibition [June 30, 1919]
- Myrrha and Strephon [July 1919]
- The House [c. July 16, 1919]
- Monody on the Late King Alcohol [August 1919]
- The Pensive Swain [October 1919]
- The City [October 1919]
- Oct 17, 1919 [October 1919]
- On Collaboration [October 20, 1919]
- To Edward John Moreton Drax Plunkett, Eighteenth Baron Dunsany [November 1919]
- Wisdom [November 1919]
- Birthday Lines to Margfred Galbraham [November 1919]
- The Nightmare Lake [December 1919]
- Bells [December 11, 1919]
- January [January 1920]
- To Phillis [January 1920]
- Tryout's Lament for the Vanished Spider [January 1920]
- Ad Scribam [February 1920]
- On Reading Lord Dunsany's Book of Wonder [March 1920]
- To a Dreamer [April 25, 1920]
- Cindy: Scrub Lady in a State Street Skyscraper [June 1920]
- The Poet's Rash Excuse [July 1920]
- With a Copy of Wilde's Fairy Tales [July 1920]
- Ex-Poet's Reply [July? 1920]
- To Two Epgephi [July? 1920]
- On Religion [August 1920]
- The Voice [August 1920]
- On a Grecian Colonnade in a Park [August 20, 1920]
- The Dream [September 1920]

- October 1 [October 1920]
- To S.S.L.—Oct 17, 1920 [October 1920]
- Christmas [November 1920]
- To Alfred Galpin, Esq. [November? 1920]
- Theobaldian Aestivation [November 11, 1920]
- S.S.L.: Christmas 1920 [December? 1920]
- On Receiving a Portraiture of Mrs. Berkeley, ye Poetess [December 25, 1920]
- The Prophecy of Capys Secundus [January 11, 1921]
- To a Youth [February 1921]
- To Mr. Hoag [February 1921]
- The Pathetick History of Sir Wilful Wildrake [Spring? 1921]
- On the Return of Maurice Winter Moe, Esq., to the Pedagogical Profession [June 1921]
- Medusa: A Portrait [November 29, 1921]
- To Mr. Galpin [December 1921]
- Sir Thomas Tryout [December 1921]
- On a Poet's Ninety-first Birthday [February 10, 1922]
- Simplicity: A Poem [c. May 18, 1922]
- To Saml: Loveman, Gent. [Summer? 1922]
- Plaster-All [August? 1922]
- To Zara [August 31, 1922]
- To Damon [November? 1922]
- Waste Paper [late 1922? early 1923?]
- To Rheinhart Kleiner, Esq. [January 1923]
- Chloris and Damon [January 1923]
- To Mr. Hoag [February? 1923]
- To Endymion [April? 1923]
- The Feast [May 1923]
- On Marblehead [July 10, 1923]
- To Mr. Baldwin, on Receiving a Picture of Him in a Rural Bower [September 29, 1923]
- Lines for Poets' Night at the Scribblers' Club [October? 1923]
- On a Scene in Rural Rhode Island [November 8, 1923]
- Damon and Lycë [December 13, 1923]
- To Mr. Hoag [c. February 3, 1924]
- On the Pyramids [c. February 1924]
- Stanzas on Samarkand I-III [February–March 1924]

- Providence [September 26, 1924]
- On The Thing in the Woods by Harper Williams [c. November 29, 1924]
- Solstice [December 25, 1924]
- To Saml Loveman, Esq. [c. January 14, 1925]
- To George Kirk, Esq. [January 18, 1925]
- My Favourite Character [January 31, 1925]
- On the Double-R Coffee House [February 1, 1925]
- To Mr. Hoag [c. February 10, 1925]
- The Cats [February 15, 1925]
- On Rheinhart Kleiner Being Hit by an Automobile [c. February 16, 1925]
- To Xanthippe, on Her Birthday—March 16, 1925 [March 1925]
- Primavera [April 1925]
- To Frank Belknap Long on His Birthday [April? 1925]
- A Year Off [July 24, 1925]
- To an Infant [August 26, 1925]
- On a Politician [c. October 24–27, 1925]
- On a Room for Rent [c. October 24–27, 1925]
- October 2 [October 30, 1925]
- To George Willard Kirk, Gent., of Chelsea-Village, in New-York, upon His Birthday, Novr. 25, 1925 [November 24, 1925]
- On Old Grimes by Albert Gorton Greene [December 1925]
- Festival [December 1925]
- To Jonathan Hoag [February 10, 1926]
- Hallowe'en in a Suburb [March 1926]
- In Memoriam: Oscar Incoul Verelst of Manhattan: 1920-1926 [c. June 28, 1926]
- The Return [December 1926]
- Εις Σφιγγην [December 1926]
- Hedone [January 3, 1927]
- To Miss Beryl Hoyt [February 1927]
- To Jonathan E. Hoag, Esq. [February? 1927]
- On J.F. Roy Erford [June 18, 1927]
- On Ambrose Bierce [c. June 1927]
- On Cheating the Post Office [c. August 14, 1927]
- On Newport, Rhode Island [September 17, 1927]
- The Absent Leader [October 12, 1927]

- Ave atque Vale [October 18, 1927]
- To a Sophisticated Young Gentleman [December 15, 1928]
- The Wood [January 1929]
- An Epistle to the Rt. Honble Maurce Winter Moe, Esq. [July 1929]
- Stanzas on Samarkand IV [November 8, 1929]
- Lines upon the Magnates of the Pulp [November 1929]
- The Outpost [November 26, 1929]
- The Ancient Track [November 26, 1929]
- The Messenger [November 30, 1929]
- The East India Brick Row [December 12, 1929]
- The Fungi From Yuggoth [December 27, 1929 – 4 January 30]
  - I. The Book
  - II. Pursuit
  - III. The Key
  - IV. Recognition
  - V. Homecoming
  - VI. The Lamp
  - VII. Zaman's Hill
  - VIII. The Port
  - IX. The Courtyard
  - X. The Pigeon-Flyers
  - XI. The Well
  - XII. The Howler
  - XIII. Hesperia
  - XIV. Star-Winds
  - XV. Antarktos
  - XVI. The Window
  - XVII. A Memory
  - XVIII. The Gardens of Yin
  - XIX. The Bells
  - XX. Night-Gaunts
  - XXI. Nyarlathotep
  - XXII. Azathoth
  - XXIII. Mirage
  - XXIV. The Canal

- XXV. St. Toad's
- XXVI. The Familiars
- XXVII. The Elder Pharos
- XXVIII. Expectancy
- XXIX. Nostalgia
- XXX. Background
- XXXI. The Dweller
- XXXII. Alienation
- XXXIII. Harbour Whistles
- XXXIV. Recapture [November 1929]
- XXXV. Evening Star
- XXXVI. Continuity
- Veteropinguis Redivivus [Summer 1930?]
- To a Young Poet in Dunedin [c. May 29, 1931]
  - FUNGI from YUGGOTH, 6. Nyarlathotep and 7. Azathoth. Verses printed in Jan. 1931 WEIRD TALES.
- On an Unspoil'd Rural Prospect [August 30, 1931]
- Bouts Rimés [May 23, 1934]
  - Beyond Zimbabwe
  - The White Elephant
- Anthem of the Kappa Alpha Tau [c. August 7, 1934]
- Edith Miniter [September 10, 1934]
- Little Sam Perkins [c. September 17, 1934]
- Metrical Example [February 27, 1935]
- Dead Passion's Flame [Summer 1935]
- Arcadia [Summer 1935]
- Lullaby for the Dionne Quintuplets [Summer 1935]
- The Odes of Horace: Book III, IX [January 22, 1936]
- In a Sequester'd Providence Churchyard Where Once Poe Walk'd [August 8, 1936]
- To Mr. Finlay, upon His Drawing for Mr. Bloch's Tale, "The Faceless God" [c. November 30, 1936]
- To Clark Ashton Smith, Esq., upon His Phantastick Tales, Verses, Pictures, and Sculptures [c. December 11, 1936]
- The Decline and Fall of a Man of the World [n.d.]
- Epigrams [n.d.]
- Gaudeamus [n.d.]

- The Greatest Law [n.d.]
- Life's Mystery [n.d.]
- On Mr. L. Phillips Howard's Profound Poem Entitled "Life's Mystery" [n.d.]
- Nathicana [n.d.]
- On an Accomplished Young Linguist [n.d.]
- "The Poetical Punch" Pushed from His Pedestal [n.d.]
- The Road to Ruin [n.d.]
- Saturnalia [n.d.]
- Sonnet Study [n.d.]
- Sors Poetae [n.d.]
- To Samuel Loveman, Esq. [n.d.]
- To "The Scribblers" [n.d.]
- Verses Designed to Be Sent by a Friend of the Author to His Brother-in-Law on New Year's Day [n.d.]
- Christmas Greetings [n.d.]
  - To Eugene B. Kuntz, et al.
  - To Laurie A. Sawyer
  - To Sonia H. Greene
  - To Rheinhart Kleiner
  - To Felis
  - To Annie E.P. Gamwell
  - To Felis

Philosophical works

- The Crime of the Century (1915)
- The Renaissance of Manhood (1915)
- Liquor and Its Friends (1915)
- More Chain Lightning (1915)
- Old England and the "Hyphen" (1916)
- Revolutionary Mythology (1916)
- The Symphonic Ideal (1916)
- Editors Note to McGavacks "Genesis of the Revolutionary War" (1917)
- A Remarkable Document (1917)
- At the Root (1918)
- Merlinus Redivivus (1918)
- Time and Space (1918)
- Anglo Saxondom (1918)
- Americanism (1919)
- The League (1919)
- Bolshevism (1919)
- Idealism and Materialism – A Reflection (1919)
- Life for Humanity's Sake (1920)
- In Defence of "Dagon" (1921)
- Nietzscheism and Realism (1922)
- East and West Harvard Conservatism (1922)
- The Materialist Today (1926)
- Some Causes of Self-Immolation (1931)
- Some Repetitions on the Times (1933)
- Heritage or Modernism: Common Sense in Art Forms (1935)
- Objections to Orthodox Communism (1936)

Scientific works

- The Art of Fusion, Melting Pudling & Casting (1899)
- Chemistry, 4 volumes (1899)
- A Good Anaesthetic (1899)
- The Railroad Review (1901)
- The Moon (1903)
- The Scientific Gazette (1903–04)
- Astronomy/The Monthly Almanack (1903–04)
- The Rhode Island Journal of Astronomy (1903–07)
- Annals of the Providence Observatory (1904)
- Providence Observatory Forecast (1904)
- The Science Library, 3 volumes (1904)
- Astronomy articles for The Pawtuxet Valley Gleaner (1906)
- Astronomy articles for The Providence Tribune (1906–08)
- Third Annual Report of the Providence Meteorological Station (1906)
- Celestial Objects for All (1907)
- Astronomical Notebook (1909–15)
- Astronomy articles for The Providence Evening News (1914–18)
- "Bickerstaffe" articles from The Providence Evening News (1914)
- "Science versus Charlatanry" (September 9, 1914)
- "The Falsity of Astrology" (October 10, 1914)
- "Astrology and the Future" (October 13, 1914)
- "Delavan's Comet and Astrology" (October 26, 1914)
- "The Fall of Astrology" (December 17, 1914)
- Astronomy articles for The Asheville Gazette-News (1915)
- Editor's Note to MacManus' "The Irish and the Fairies" (1916)
- The Truth about Mars (1917)
- The Cancer of Superstition (1926)

Miscellaneous writings

- A Task for Amateur Journalists (1914)
- Departments of Public Criticism (1914–19)
- What Is Amateur Journalism? (1915)
- Consolidations Autopsy (1915)
- Consolidation's Autopsy (1915)
- The Amateur Press (1915)
- The Morris Faction (1915)
- For President – Leo Fritter (1915)
- Introducing Mr. Chester Pierce Munroe (1915)
- The Question of the Day (1915)
- Random Notes, from The Conservative (1915)
- Editorials, from The Conservative (1915)
- Finale (1915)
- New Department Proposed: Instruction for the New Recruit (1915)
- Amateur Notes (1915)
- Some Political Phases (1915)
- Introducing Mr. John Russell (1915)
- In a Major Key (1915)
- The Conservative and His Critics (1915)
- The Dignity of Journalism (1915)
- The Youth of Today (1915)
- An Impartial Spectator (1915)
- Symphony and Stress (1915)
- Little Journeys to the Homes of Prominent Amateurs (1915)
- Reports of the First Vice-President (1915–16)
- Systematic Instruction in the United (1915–16)
- Introducing Mr. James T. Pyke (1916)
- Editorial, from The Providence Amateur (1916)
- United Amateur Press Association: Exponent of Amateur Journalism (1916)
- Among the New-Comers (1916)
- Among the Amateurs (1916)

- Concerning "Persia – In Europe" (1917)
- Amateur Standards (1917)
- A Request (1917)
- A Reply to The Lingerer (1917)
- Editorially (1917)
- News Notes (1917)
- The United's Problem (1917)
- Little Journeys to the Homes of Prominent Amateurs (1917)
- President's Messages, from The United Amateur (1917–18)
- Comment (1918)
- Les Mouches Fantastiques (1918)
- Amateur Criticism (1918)
- The United: 1917–1918 (1918)
- The Amateur Press Club (1918)
- Helene Hoffman Cole – Littérateur (1919)
- Trimmings (1919)
- For Official Editor – Anne Tillery Renshaw (1919)
- Amateurdom (1919)
- Looking Backward (1920)
- For What Does the United Stand? (1920)
- Untitled, from The Tryout (1920)
- Editor's Note to Loveman's "A Scene for Macbeth" (1920)
- Amateur Journalism – Its Possible Needs and Betterment (1920)
- The Pseudo-United (1920)
- Untitled Fragments, from The United Amateur (1920–1)
- Editorials, from The United Amateur (1920–5)
- News Notes (1920–5)
- What Amateur Journalism and I Have Done for Each Other (1921)
- Lucubrations Lovecraftian (1921)
- The Vivisector (1921–23)
- The Haverhill Convention (1921–23)
- The Convention Banquet (1921–23)
- "Rainbow" Called Best First Issue (1922)
- President's Messages, from The National Amateur (1922–23)
- Rursus Adsumus (1923)

- Bureau of Critics (1923)
- Random Notes, from The Conservative (1923)
- The President's Annual Report (1923)
- A Matter of Uniteds (1927)
- The Convention (1930)
- Bureau of Critics (1932–36)
- Mrs. Miniter – Estimates and Recollections (1934)
- Dr. Eugene B. Kuntz (1935)
- Some Current Motives and Practices (1936)
- Literary Review (1936)
- Defining the "Ideal" Paper (1936)
- Report of the Executive Judges (1936)
- Metrical Regularity (1915)
- The Allowable Rhyme (1915)
- The Proposed Authors Union (1916)
- The Vers Libre Epidemic (1917)
- Poesy (1918)
- The Despised Pastoral (1918)
- The Literature of Rome (1918)
- The Simple Spelling Mania (1918)
- The Case for Classicism (1919)
- Literary Composition (1919)
- Winifred Virginia Jackson: A Different Poetess (1921)
- Ars Gratia Artis (1921)
- The Poetry of Lilian Middleton (1922)
- Lord Dunsany and His Work (1922)
- Rudis Indigestaque Moles (1923)
- Introduction to Hoags Poetical Works (1923)
- In the Editors Study (1923)
- Random Notes on Philistine-Grecian Controversy (1923)
- Review of Ebony and Crystal by Clark Ashton Smith (1923)
- The Professional Incubus (1924)
- The Omnipresent Philistine (1924)
- "The Work of Frank Belknap Long, Jr." (1924)
- Supernatural Horror in Literature (1925–1927)

- Preface to Bullens White Fire (1927)
- Preface to Symmes Old World Footprints (1928)
- Notes on Alias Peter Marchall by A. F. Lorenz (1929?)
- Notes on Verse Technique (1932)
- Foreword to Kuntzs Thoughts and Pictures (1932)
- Notes on Weird Fiction (1933)
- Weird Story Plots (1933)
- Notes on Writing Weird Fiction (1934)
- Some Notes on Interplanetary Fiction (1935)
- What Belongs in Verse (1935)
- Suggestions for a Reading Guide (1936)
- The Trip of Theobald (1927)
- Vermont – A First Impression (1927)
- Observations on Several Parts of America (1928)
- An Account of a Trip to the Fairbanks House (1929)
- Travels in the Provinces of America (1929)
- An Account of a Visit to Charleston (1930)
- An Account of Charleston (1930)
- A Description of the Town of Quebeck (1930–31)
- European Glimpses (1932) (revision of a Sonia Greene's journey report)
- Some Dutch Footprints in New England (1933)
- Homes and Shrines of Poe (1934)
- The Unknown City in the Ocean (1934)
- Charleston (1936)
- The Brief Autobiography of an Inconsequential Scribbler (1919)
- Within the Gates (1921)
- A Confession of Unfaith (1922)
- Diary (1925)
- Commercial Blurbs (1925)
- Cats and Dogs (1926)
- Notes on Hudson Valley History (1929)
- Autobiography of Howard Phillips Lovecraft (1930–...)
- Correspondence between Wilson Shepherd and R. H. Barlow (1932)
- In Memoriam: Henry St. Claire Whitehead (1932)
- Some Notes on a Nonentity (1933)

- In Memoriam: Robert Ervin Howard (1936)
- Commonplace Book (1919–1935)
- Death Diary (1937)

L . & . D
edition

L.&.D
edition

Printed in Great Britain
by Amazon

45705004R00036